The Case of
The Battling Ball Clubs

by **Dan Cohen** ✦ *Pictures by* **George Overlie**

CAROLRHODA BOOKS
MINNEAPOLIS, MINNESOTA U.S.A.

1 2 3 4 5 6 7 8 9 10 85 84 83 82 81 80 79

"Grr!" said Polly. "Grrrrrrr! Grr! Grr! Grr!"

"What's that all about, Polly?" asked Officer Grover Greenwood. He and Polly were standing by home plate at the Spring Grove ball park. They were watching Polly's older sister, Ruth-ann, practice swinging her new baseball bat.

Ruthann took a time-out. "Polly's practicing her growl," she told Officer Greenwood. "For our team. We're playing in the big game to-morrow for the Spring Grove Growlers."

"That's right," said Buzz Walters, the Growl-ers' manager. "Polly and Ruthann are two of our best players. I'm counting on them for to-morrow's big game with the Westend Warriors."

"Grr!" said Polly. "Grr! Grr! Go Growlers!"

"That should be a pretty exciting game," said Officer Greenwood. "There's a real battle between your team and the Warriors, isn't there?"

"Has been for years," said Buzz Walters. "Spike Bascom, the Warriors' manager, lives almost next door to me. But we haven't been friendly for years. His son, Waldo, is the star pitcher for the Warriors. He won't be playing in the big game tomorrow, though. He hurt his arm. That sure hasn't made Spike any easier to get along with."

"The field looks kind of wet," said Officer Greenwood. "I hope it'll be in good shape for the game tomorrow. You know, that thunderstorm last night was pretty bad. It even knocked

out the electricity for a couple of hours—from midnight until the storm was over."

"It was bad, all right," said Buzz. "But the field should be dry in plenty of time for the game."

Just then someone came running up, shouting and waving his arms.

"Arrest that man! Arrest that man!" he yelled. It was Spike Bascom.

"Officer, I want you to arrest that man. Buzz Walters broke into my house last night and took my autographed picture of Babe Ruth!"

"What are you talking about, Bascom?"
asked Buzz.

"You know exactly what I'm talking about, Walters," said Spike Bascom. "Last night during the storm, you broke my den window. You climbed in and took one of my most prized possessions. I've had that autographed picture of Babe Ruth ever since I was in high school. Now it's gone. Officer Greenwood, that man should be in jail!"

"Now wait a minute, Spike. Why do you think Buzz would want to take that picture?"

"He took it to get me all riled up for the game tomorrow, that's why. He's hoping I'll make a mistake and lose the game. Otherwise he knows he hasn't got a chance to win!"

"Can you prove he did it?" asked Officer Greenwood.

"I *know* he did it!" cried Spike. "He's the only one in Spring Grove low enough to pull something like this. Besides, he's plenty stupid, too. He threw his own baseball shoe through my window! That big gunboat is still sitting right in the middle of my den. Come on, I'll show you."

Spike didn't live far from the field, so they all walked to his house with him. When they got there, Waldo was waiting in the den. The signs of the break-in were all around. There was the shoe in the middle of the room. There was an empty spot on the wall where Spike's prize picture had been. And there was the window with a big hole in it.

"Can you tell us exactly what happened, Spike?" asked Officer Greenwood.

"Well, I had gone to bed kind of early last night, before the storm started. I was sleeping very soundly. Then sometime in the middle of the night, Waldo came in and woke me up. He

said he'd heard a noise downstairs like breaking glass. Isn't that right, Waldo?"

"Yup," said Waldo.

"Well, I heard the rain and thunder outside.

I thought that the storm might have made the
noise Waldo heard. I wanted to check. So I got
up and felt around in the dark for my robe and

slippers. There weren't any lights 'cause of the
storm. Isn't that right, Waldo?"

"Yup," said Waldo.

"How do you know this shoe belongs to Buzz Walters, Spike?" asked Officer Greenwood.

"First of all, look at the size of the thing. Walters has got the biggest feet in three counties. And then, without even picking it up, I can read his name written right in it."

"Seems kind of funny that someone would throw his own shoe with his name on it through a window if he didn't want to get caught," said Polly.

"Anyone could have gotten that shoe out of my locker. Spike and Waldo are in and out of the locker room just as much as I am," said Buzz.

"There's something else funny about this shoe," said Ruthann, picking it up. "It's dry. But if someone had been wearing it during the

storm, or even carrying it, it would probably
still be wet or muddy."

"Very interesting," said Officer Greenwood. "Polly, what are you doing?" he asked. Polly was down on her hands and knees, crawling around on the rug.

"Looking for mud," said Polly. "The thief would have gotten mud or water on the rug

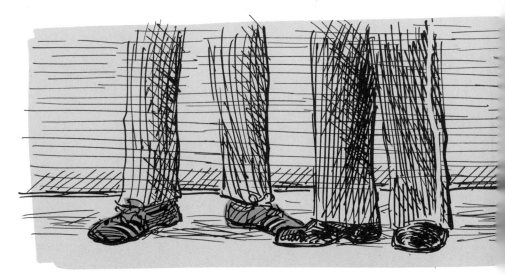

when he crossed the room to get the picture, wouldn't he?"

"Well, he certainly would have, Polly," said the officer. "Good thinking! But watch out for broken glass down there."

"Oh, it's okay," said Polly. "There isn't any glass."

"I think I'll go outside and have a look around," said Ruthann suddenly. She ran around to the side door and let herself out. Soon they could see her outdoors under the den window, looking closely at the ground.

"This is strange," she called. "There are no footprints out here! Of course, I suppose the rain could have washed them out. The ground's just covered with broken glass, though."

"Girls, I'm very lucky to have such good help," said Officer Greenwood. "I think you've both given me an idea."

Ruthann hurried back inside. "What is it, Officer Greenwood?" she asked.

"Well, there's something strange about the broken glass," said Officer Greenwood. "Waldo, have you or your dad moved anything or cleaned up since you found the picture missing?"

"Nope," said Waldo.

"That's very odd, because there's no broken glass inside," said Officer Greenwood. "The broken glass is outdoors. If the shoe had been thrown from outside, glass would have broken all over the room. Not only that, but there is no mud on the shoe or the rug. That tells me that nobody climbed in from outside at all. Whoever broke the glass, broke it from the inside. That means that it was someone who was in the house all the time."

"You mean it could have been either Spike or Waldo?" asked Ruthann.

"That's right," said Officer Greenwood. "I think we can clear this up pretty quickly. Waldo, about what time did you wake up your dad?"

Waldo swallowed hard. "Uhhh—'bout two,"
he said.

"Right after you heard the breaking glass?"

"Yup," said Waldo.

"Raining pretty hard then?"

"Yup."

"Waldo, how were you so sure what time you woke your dad?"

Waldo hesitated. "Um—the clock radio next to my bed," he said quickly. "When the noise woke me up, I looked at it right away. It said two o'clock."

"It couldn't have!" said Officer Greenwood. "A clock radio runs on electricity. But the electricity was off during the storm last night. It went off at midnight. It didn't go back on until after the storm was over at two o'clock. Yet you said it was still raining when you woke

up. If that's true, then the clock would have shown around midnight."

Waldo looked like he wanted to sink into the floor.

"Waldo, I'm afraid you haven't been telling us the truth. Your story doesn't hold up. I think you had to make up something quickly to hide the truth about what you really did. You waited until your dad was asleep. You broke the window and took the picture. Then you woke your dad with the story about the breaking glass. Isn't that true?"

When Waldo whispered "yup," he could hardly be heard.

"Why did you do it, son?" asked Spike. "Why did you take my Babe Ruth picture? I know you're jealous, 'cause he's better than Rod Carew and Hank Aaron and all the rest of those modern so-called stars you're always talking about. But that's no reason to take my Babe Ruth!"

"Oh, dad, I didn't hurt that old picture. I've got it right up in my room," said Waldo. "I just wanted to get Mr. Walters in trouble. I thought if he was all upset he'd lose the game tomorrow. I wanted to be sure our team won. If we lost—well—people would think it was my fault for not playing. They'd say I let down the team."

"Oh, Waldo, you big dummy!" said Spike. "Everybody knows you hurt your arm. They know you can't help that. The whole thing's ridiculous! Officer, I apologize. And I apologize to you, too, Walters. And so does Waldo. Don't you, Waldo?"

"Yup," said Waldo.

"Waldo, 'yup' isn't good enough this time," said Spike.

"I apologize, Mr. Walters. I did a dumb thing. It won't happen again."

"That's all right, Waldo. We all make mistakes. I don't hold it against you," said Buzz.

"Neither do we," said Ruthann. "But I'm afraid our team's still going to beat your team tomorrow, with or without you!"

And that's exactly what they did.